MARK ELF

JAZZ Interpretations

Original Etudes Based on Progression Similar to *Stella*

VOLUME 1

Mark Elf plays "The Mark Elf Custom Classic" built by Jim DeCava

1 2 3 4 5 6 7 8 9 0

Visit us on the Web at www.melbay.com — E-mail us at email@melbay.com

Contents

About the Author

Mark Elf has been on the jazz scene for over 30 years. He was born in Queens, New York in 1949 and started playing the Guitar at the age of 11. He has played and or recorded with the Jazz Giants: Dizzy Gillespie, Clark Terry, Jimmy Heath & the Heath Brothers, Wynton Marsalis & Jon Hendricks just to name a few. His first professional Jazz performance occurred around 1971 as a sideman at the Club Barron in Harlem, New York with Gloria Coleman and Etta Jones. This performance was a double bill with the George Benson Quintet.

During the 1970's he toured with Lou Donaldson, Jimmy McGriff, Groove Holmes & Charles Earland and recorded a number of albums with them. He recorded his first album as a sideman with Jimmy McGriff & Groove Holmes in 1973 on the Groove Merchant Record label entitled *Giants of the Organ Come Together*. In the late 1970's, while living in New York he also worked with Junior Cook and Bill Hardman.

In the 1980's he toured Europe with Dizzy Gillespie, Clark Terry and other jazz luminaries and also recorded his first album as a leader in 1986 entitled the *Mark Elf Trio Volume 1*.

In 1988 he recorded his second album as a leader, *The Eternal Triangle,* with Hank Jones, Jimmy Heath, Ray Drummond and Ben Riley. This album was released in 1996 on Mark's Jen Bay Record Label.

The year 1993 brought Mark his first overseas record deal with The Alerce Record Label and *The Mark Elf Trio* was recorded in Santiago, Chile. This recording was marketed to radio in 1996 and went to #7 on The Gavin Jazz Chart.

The year 1995 found Mark recording for Telarc on the Jon Hendricks CD, *Boppin' at The Blue Note*, with Wynton Marsalis, Benny Golson, Al Grey & Red Holloway. This recording went to #1 and opened up some radio doors just before the Alerce recording released in 1996.

After forming his own record company in 1995, Jen Bay Records, he stunned the record industry with hit recordings on Jazz Radio. From 1996 to 2002 all nine of his recordings had finished in the top ten on National Jazz Radio with seven of them going to #1 consecutively from 1997 to 2002.

In 1996 he joined the Jimmy Heath band and also worked with the Heath Brothers During this time the *Eternal Triangle* was released and it went to #4 on The Gavin Jazz Chart. He recorded *As We Were Saying* with the Heath Brothers for Concord Records in 1997. This same year Mark's third recording as a leader, *A Minor Scramble* was released. This was the second record for his own company and it hit #1 on The Gavin Jazz Chart. This was the first of seven consecutive chart toppers! The other six were: 1998 - *Trickynometry* (#1), 1999 - *New York Cats* (#1), 2000 - *Over The Airwaves* and *Live At Smalls* (#1), 2001 - *Swingin'* (#1) and 2002 - *Dream Steppin'* (#1).

From 1970 to the present Mark has taught guitar and theory at independent studios, colleges and universities in the USA and abroad. His clinics are recognized as some of the finest in the world as attested to by Clark Terry who hired Mark to teach at several of his jazz camps in the 1980's and 1990's. Clark said, "The students love his no nonsense practical approach. He's a great clinician."

Beside owning his own successful record label, he also owns his own publishing company. He is sought after for his lectures on "How To Succeed As An INDIE."

Presently Mark is touring with his trio performing at festivals, colleges and clubs.

Stella 1

Em7(♭5)
A7(♭9)
Cmin7
F7
Fmin7
B♭7(♭9)
E♭Maj7
E♭min7
B♭Maj7
Emin7
A7(♭9)
Dmin7
B♭min7
E♭7
FMaj7
D7(♭9)
Gmin7
C7(♭9)
Am7(♭5)
D7(♭9)

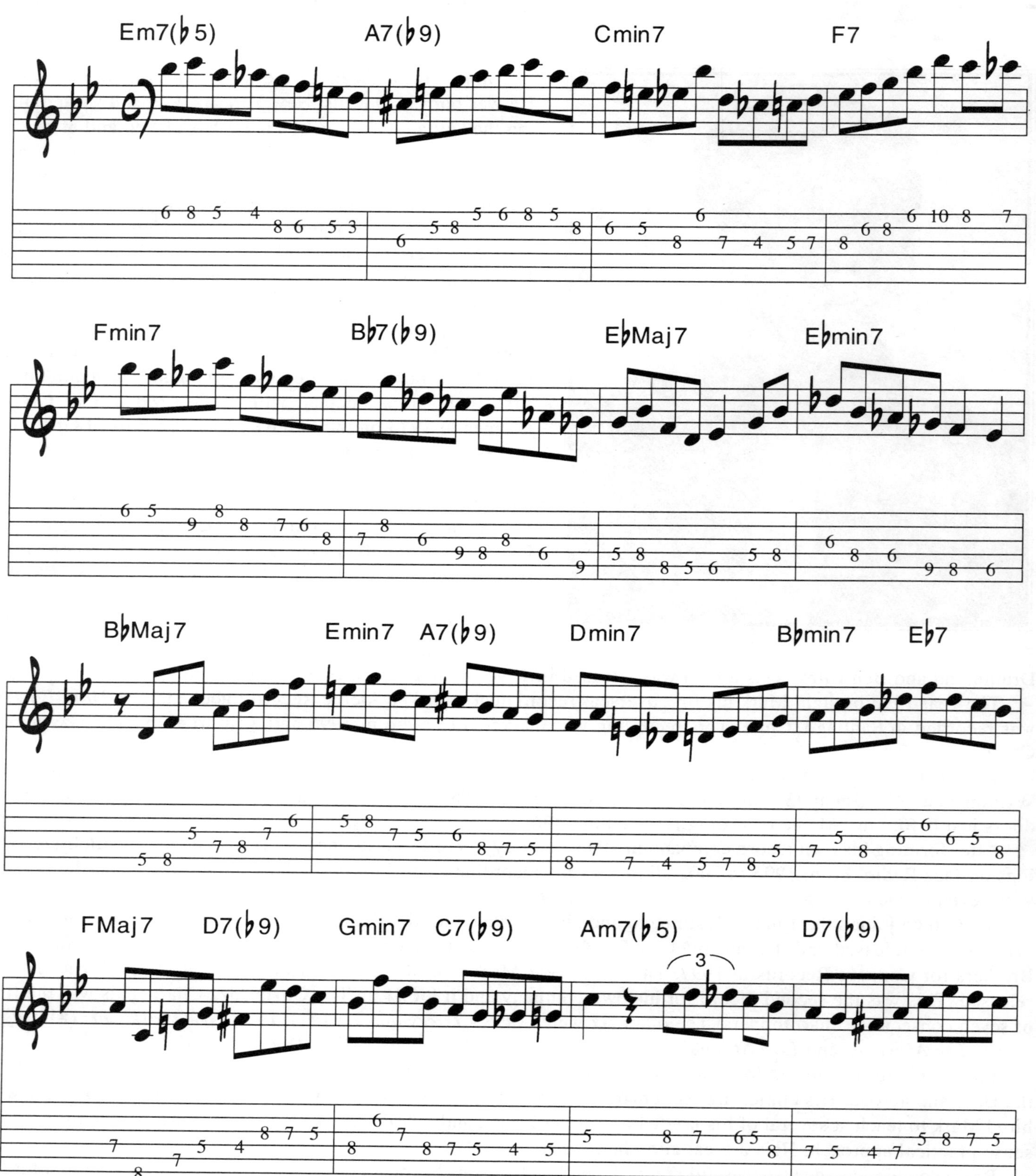

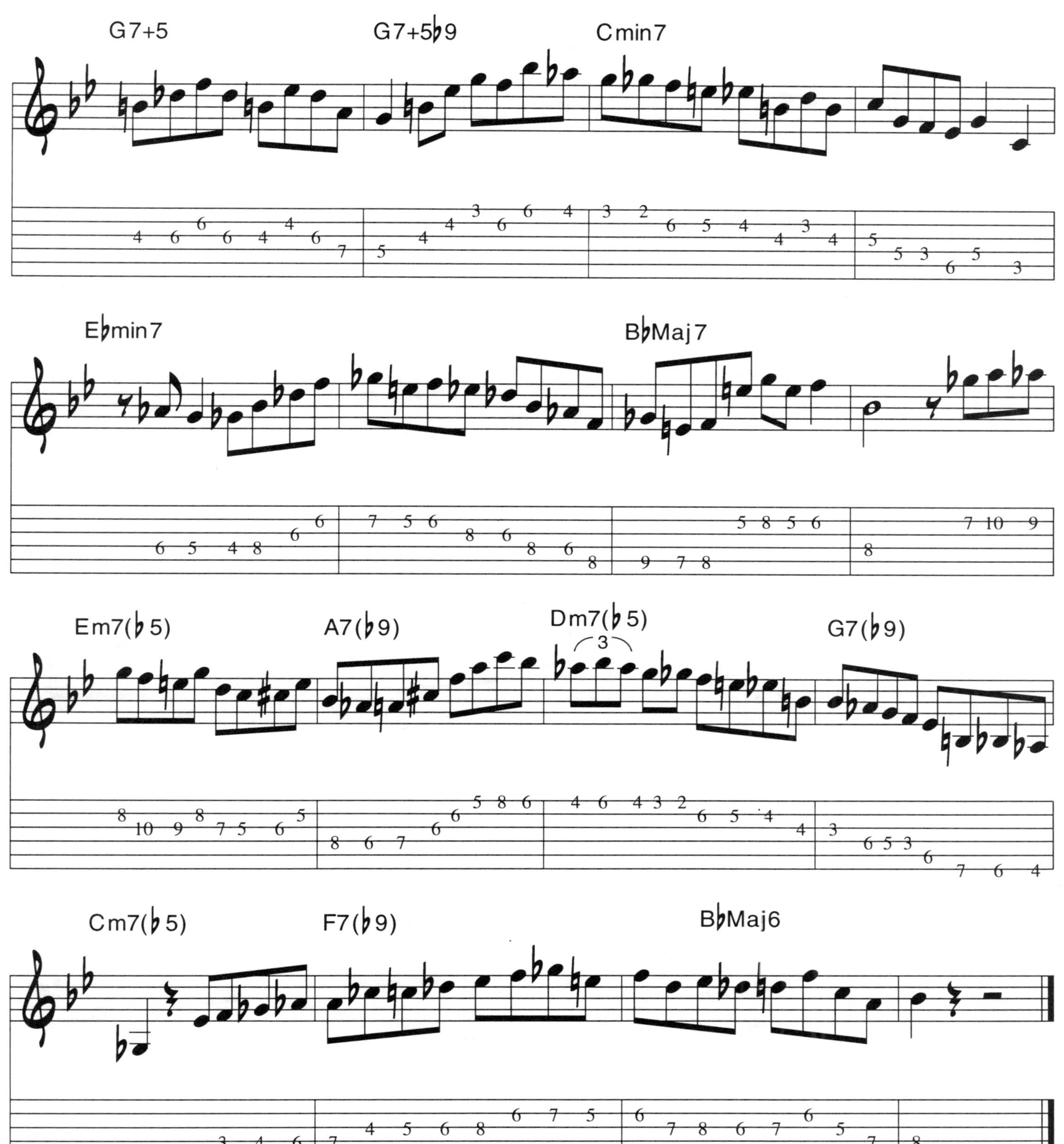

G7+5
G7+5♭9
Cmin7
E♭min7
B♭Maj7
Em7(♭5)
A7(♭9)
Dm7(♭5)
G7(♭9)
Cm7(♭5)
F7(♭9)
B♭Maj6

Stella 2

Em7(♭5)
A7(♭9)
Cmin7
F7
Fmin7
B♭7+5♭9
E♭Maj7
E♭min7
A♭7(♯11)
B♭Maj6
Emin7
A7(♭9)
Dmin7
B♭min7
E♭7
FMaj7
D7(♭9)
Gmin7
C7+5♭9
Am7(♭5)
D7(♭9)

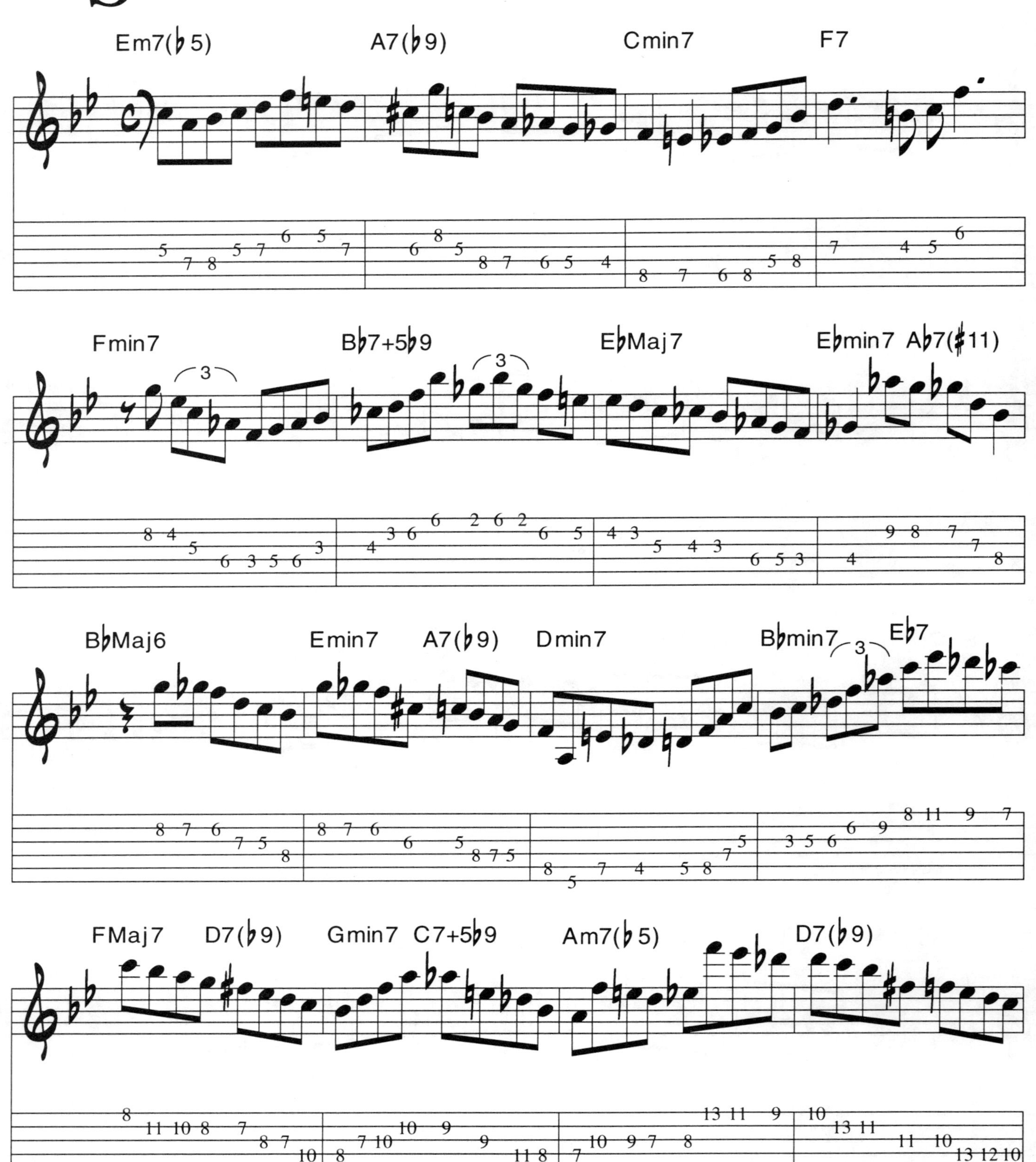

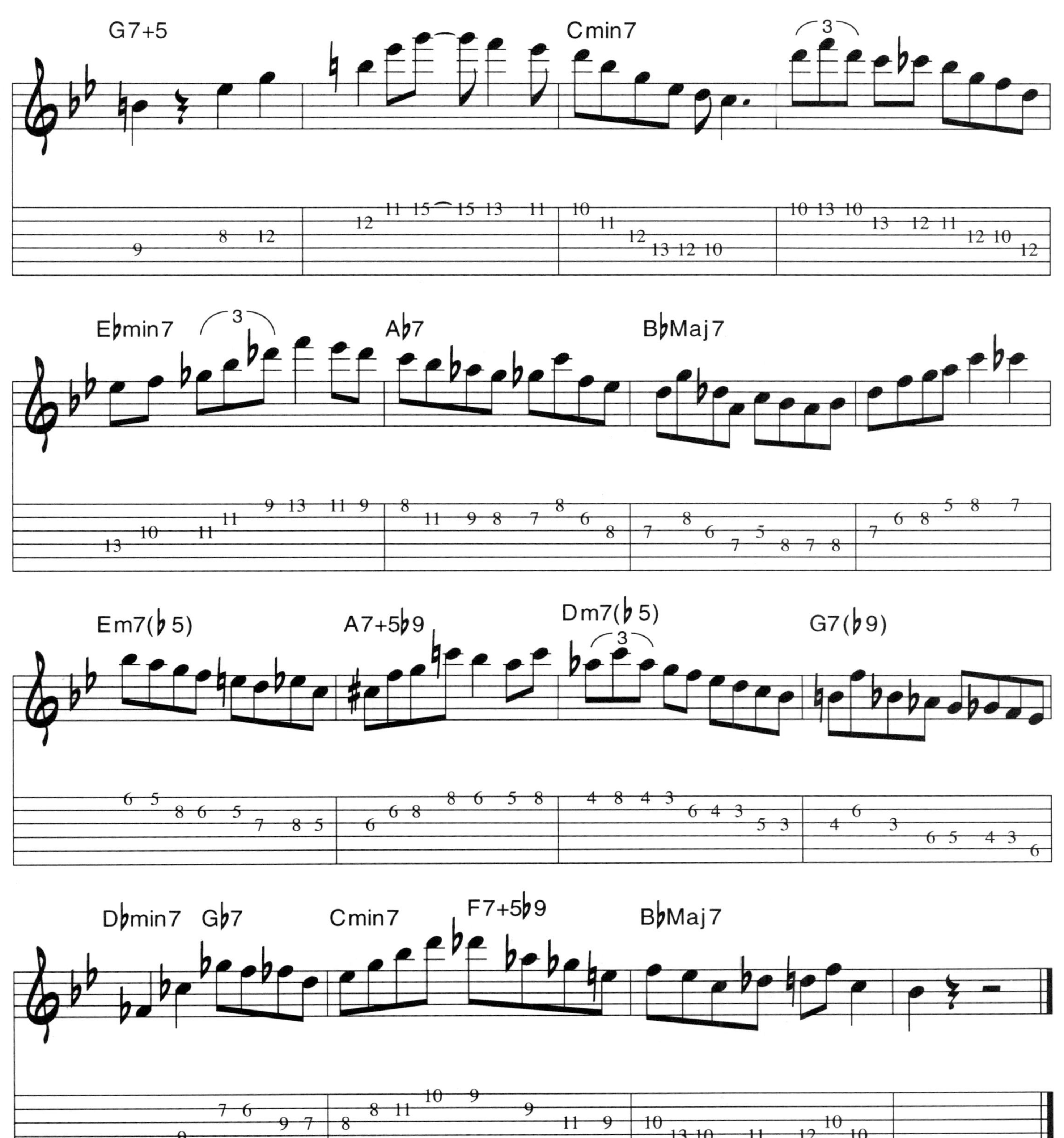
G7+5
Cmin7
E♭min7
A♭7
B♭Maj7
Em7(♭5)
A7+5♭9
Dm7(♭5)
G7(♭9)
D♭min7
G♭7
Cmin7
F7+5♭9
B♭Maj7

Stella 3

Em7(♭5)
A7(♭9)
Cmin7
F7
Fmin7
B♭7
E♭Maj7
E♭min7
A♭7
B♭Maj7
Emin7
A7(♭9)
Dmin7
B♭min7
E♭7
FMaj7
D7(♭9)
Gmin7
C7+5
Am7(♭5)
D7(♭9)

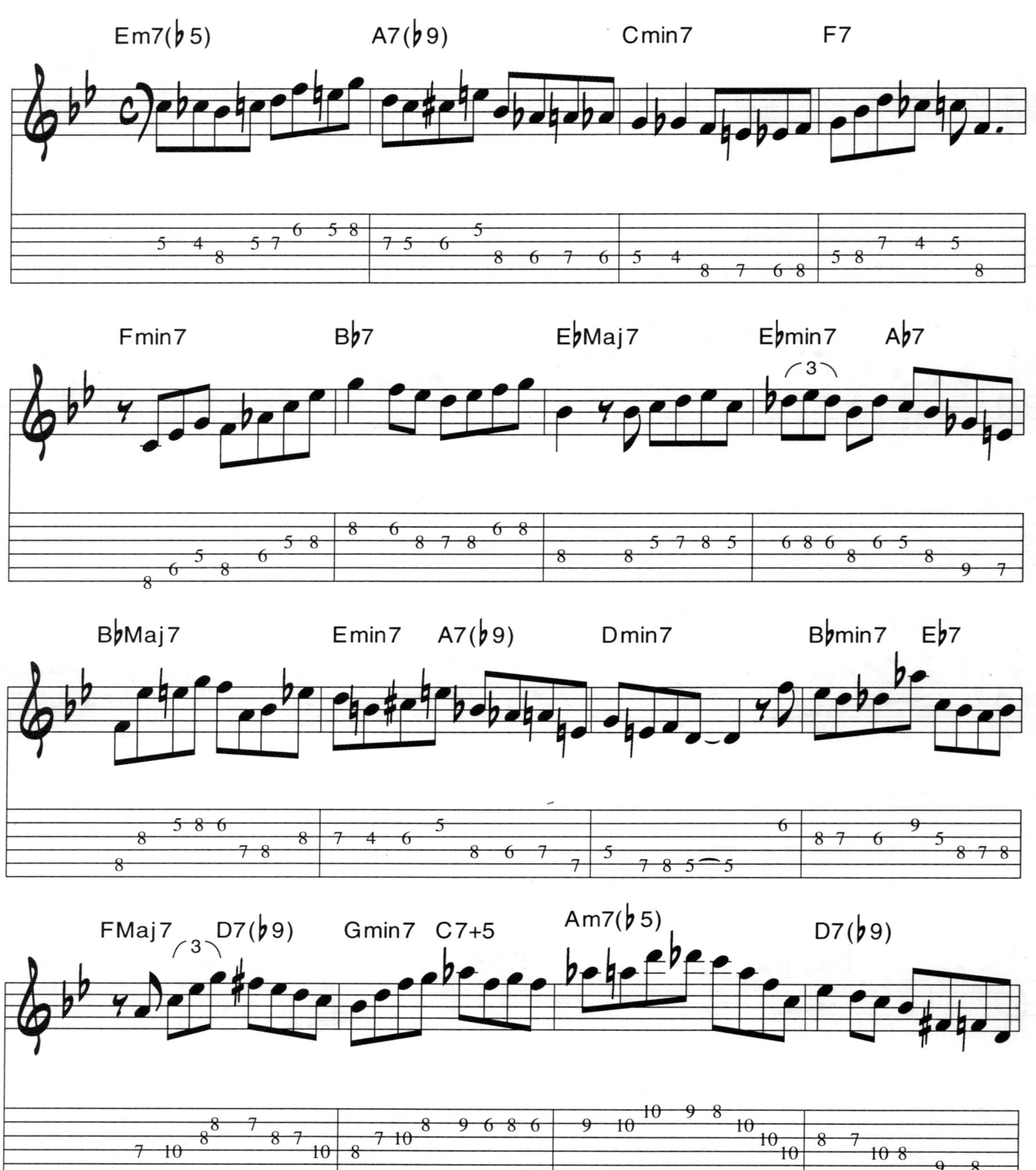

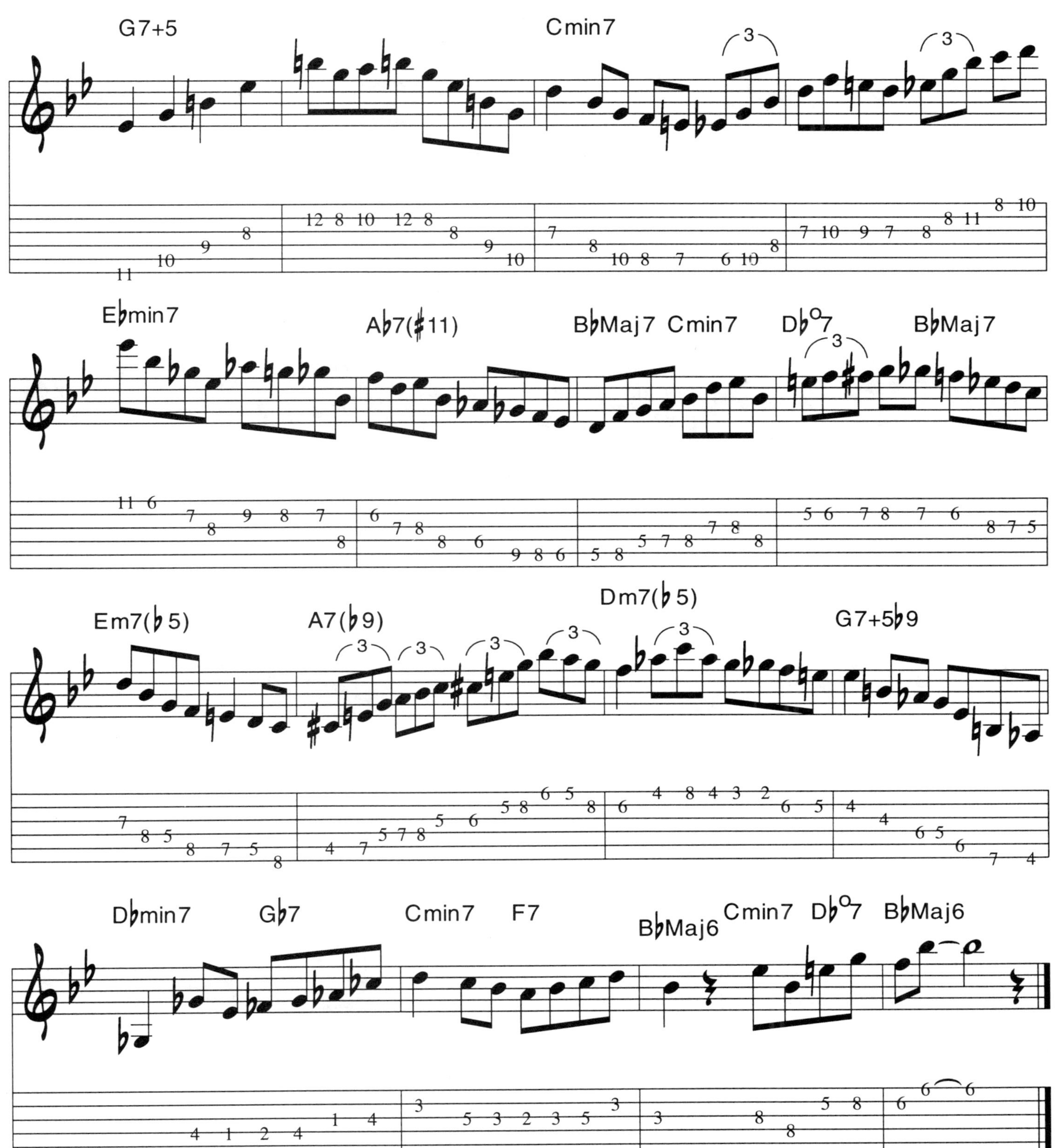
G7+5
Cmin7
E♭min7
A♭7(♯11)
B♭Maj7
Cmin7
D♭°7
B♭Maj7
Em7(♭5)
A7(♭9)
Dm7(♭5)
G7+5♭9
D♭min7
G♭7
Cmin7
F7
B♭Maj6
Cmin7
D♭°7
B♭Maj6

Stella 4

A7(♭9)
Cmin7
F7
Fmin7
B♭7(♭9)
E♭Maj6
E♭min7
A♭7
B♭Maj7
Emin7
A7
Dmin7
B♭min7
FMaj7
D7+5♭9
Gmin7
C7
Am7(♭5)
D7+5♭9

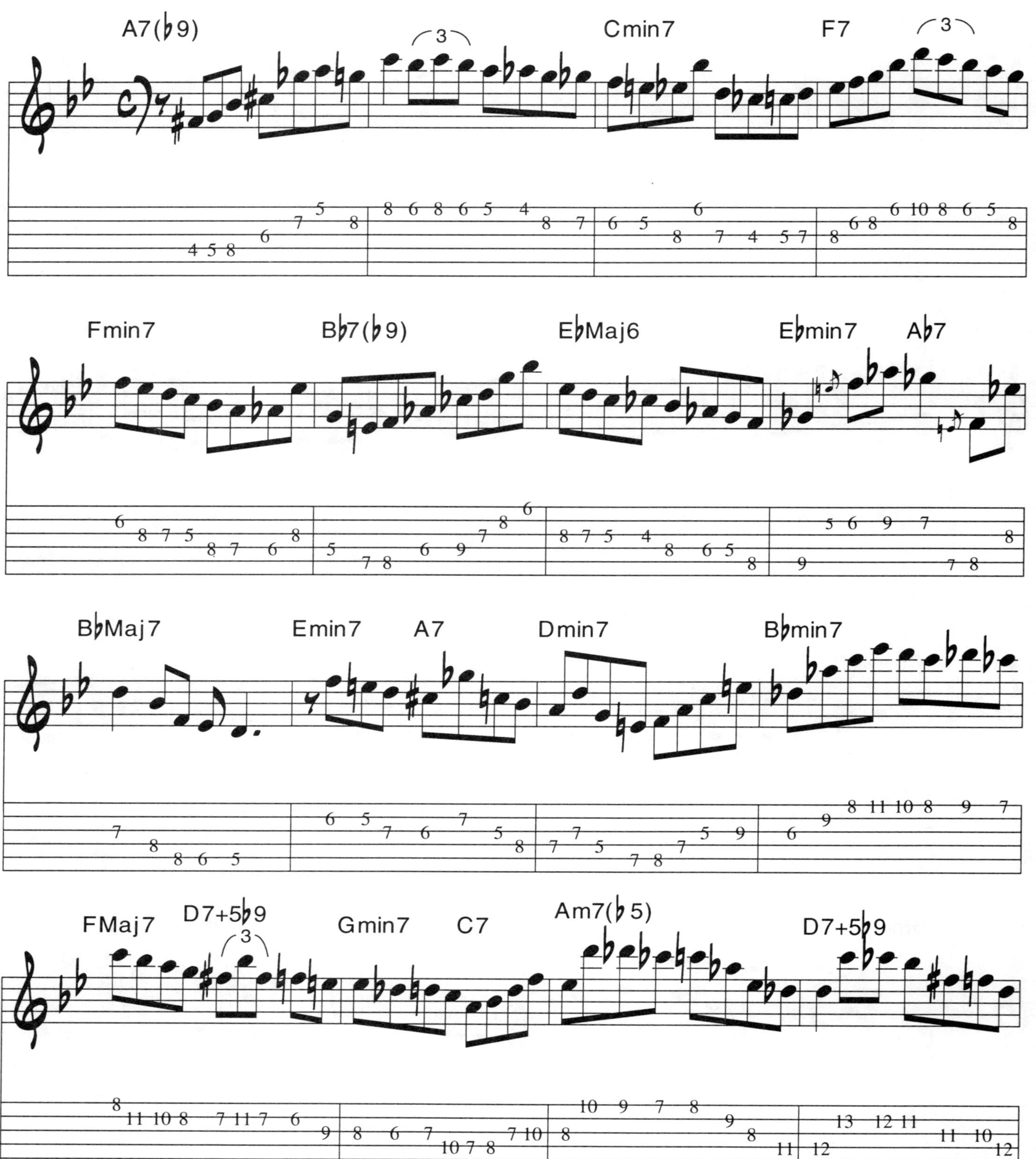

G7
G7+5♭9
Cmin7
E♭min7
A♭7
B♭Maj7
Cmin7
D♭o7
B♭Maj6
Em7(♭5)
A7(♭9)
Dm7(♭5)
G7(♭9)
D♭min7
G♭7
Cmin7
F7(♭9)
D♭7+5
B♭Maj6
Cmin7
B7
B♭Maj6

Stella 5

Em7(♭5)
A7(♭9)
3
Cmin7
F7
Fmin7
B♭7(♭9)
E♭Maj7
E♭min7
A♭7
B♭Maj7
Em7(♭5)
A7(♭9)
3
Dmin7
B♭min7
FMaj7
D7(♭9)
Gmin7
3
C7(♭9)
Am7(♭5)
D7(♭9)

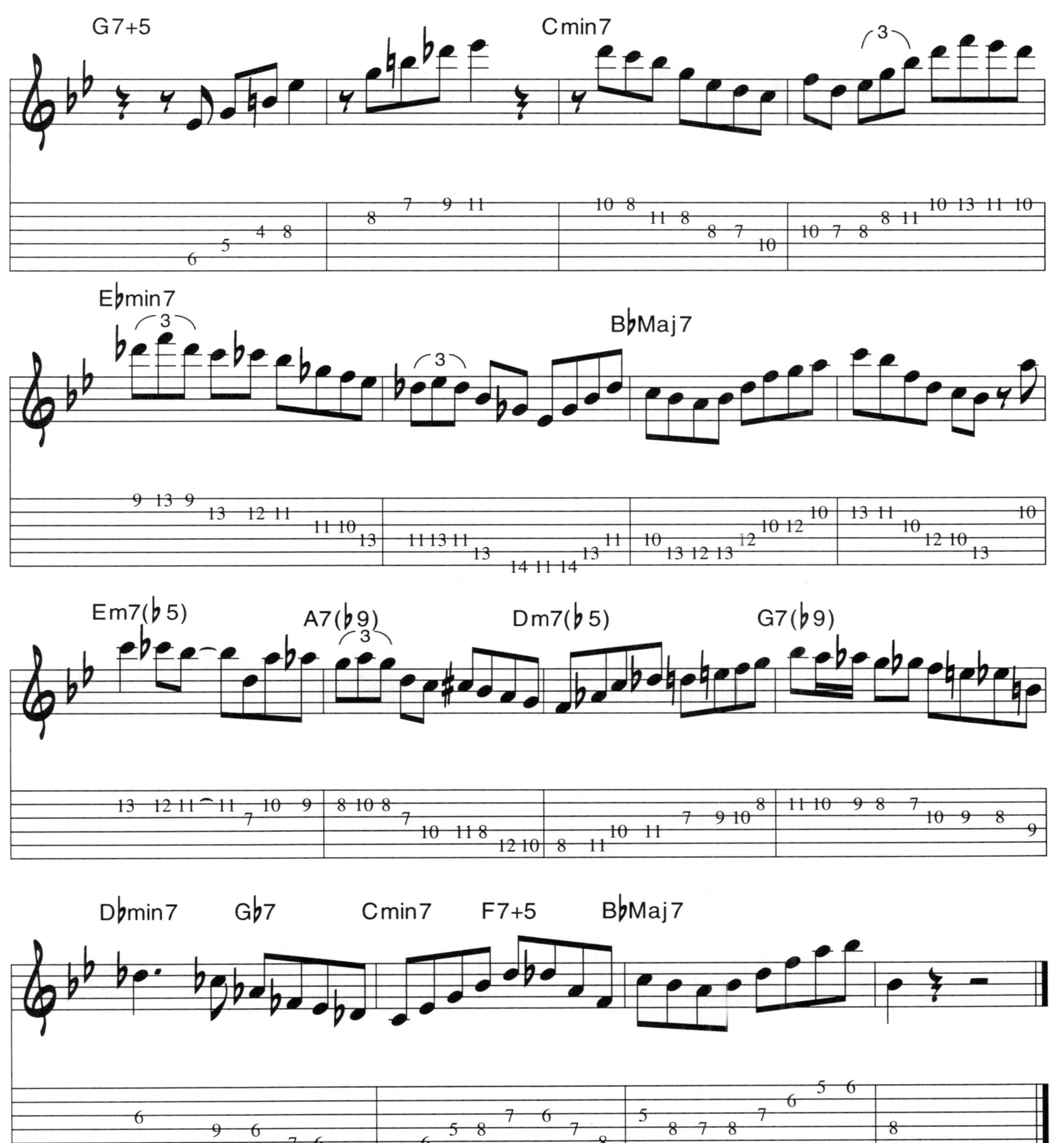
G7+5
Cmin7
E♭min7
B♭Maj7
Em7(♭5)
A7(♭9)
Dm7(♭5)
G7(♭9)
D♭min7
G♭7
Cmin7
F7+5
B♭Maj7

From left to right: Bill Hardman, Clifford Jordan, Mark Elf, Lou Donaldson, Jamil Nasser, Vernel Fournier. 1985

Tal Farlow & Mark Elf at Merkin Hall. A Tribute to Tal Farlow's 75th birthday in 1995. © R. Andrew Lepley.

Mark Elf with Dizzy Gillespie in Greece during a 1988 European Concert Tour.

From left to right: Mark Elf, Walter Booker, Bill Hardman & LeRoy Williams. The Bill Hardman Quartet at the Hartford, CT Jazz Society Concert in 1985.

Concert with Jimmy Heath. From left to right Jimmy Heath, Chip Jackson, Mark Elf. © Jazz'n Blues Photography.